TREASURED
TALES
of
CHRISTMAS

Adaptations by Deborah Apy

Table of Contents

The Night Before Christmas

Clement C. Moore

'Twas the night before Christmas, when all through the house
Not a creature was stirring, not even a mouse;
The stockings were hung by the chimney with care,
In hopes that St. Nicholas soon would be there;
The children were nestled all snug in their beds,
While visions of sugarplums danced in their heads;

And Mama in her 'kerchief, and I in my cap,
Had just settled our brains for a long winter's nap;
When out on the lawn there arose such a clatter,
I sprang from the bed to see what was the matter.
Away to the window I flew like a flash,
Tore open the shutters and threw up the sash.

The moon, on the breast of the new-fallen snow,
Gave the lustre of midday to objects below,
When what to my wondering eyes should appear,
But a miniature sleigh, and eight tiny reindeer,
With a little old driver, so lively and quick,
I knew in a moment it must be St. Nick.

More rapid than eagles his coursers they came,
And he whistled and shouted, and called them by name;
'Now, Dasher! Now, Dancer! Now, Prancer and Vixen!
On, Comet! On, Cupid! On, Donner and Blitzen!
To the top of the porch! To the top of the wall!
Now, dash away! Dash away! Dash away all!'

As dry leaves that before the wild hurricane fly,
When they meet with an obstacle, mount to the sky;
So up to the housetop the coursers they flew,
With the sleigh full of toys, and St. Nicholas, too.

And then, in a twinkling, I heard on the roof
The prancing and pawing of each little hoof —
As I drew in my head, and was turning around,
Down the chimney St. Nicholas came with a bound.

He was dressed all in fur, from his head to his foot,
And his clothes were all tarnished with ashes and soot;
A bundle of toys he had flung on his back,
And he looked like a pedlar just opening his pack.
His eyes — how they twinkled! His dimples, how merry!
His cheeks were like roses, his nose like a cherry!

His droll little mouth was drawn up like a bow,
And the beard of his chin was as white as the snow;
The stump of a pipe he held tight in his teeth,
And the smoke it encircled his head like a wreath;
He had a broad face and a little round belly
That shook, when he laughed, like a bowl full of jelly.

He was chubby and plump, a right jolly old elf,
And I laughed, when I saw him, in spite of myself;
A wink of his eye and a twist of his head,
Soon gave me to know I had nothing to dread;
He spoke not a word, but went straight to his work,
And filled all the stockings; then turned with a jerk.

And laying his finger aside of his nose,
And giving a nod, up the chimney he rose;
He sprang to his sleigh, to his team gave a whistle,
And away they all flew like the down of a thistle.
But I heard him exclaim, ere he drove out of sight,
'Happy Christmas to all, and to all a good night.'

The Friendly Beasts

Jesus our brother, strong and good,
Was humbly born in a stable rude,
And the friendly beasts around Him stood,
Jesus our brother, strong and good.

"I," said the donkey, shaggy and brown,
"I carried His mother up hill and down,
I carried her safely to Bethlehem town;
I," said the donkey, shaggy and brown.

"I," said the cow, all white and red,
"I gave Him my manger for His bed,
I gave Him my hay to pillow His head,
I," said the cow, all white and red.

"I," said the sheep, with curly horn,
"I gave Him my wool for His blanket warm,
He wore my coat on Christmas morn;
I," said the sheep, with curly horn.

"I," said the dove, from rafters high,
"Cooed Him to sleep, my mate and I,
We cooed Him to sleep, my mate and I;
I," said the dove from the rafters high.

And every beast, by some good spell,
In the stable dark was glad to tell,
Of the gift he gave Immanuel,
The gift he gave Immanuel.

Twelfth Century Carol

The Birthday

In a darkened room, four little children are sleeping soundly. Their thick, downy quilts are clutched to their chins; soft, feather pillows are plumped beneath their cheeks. Outside, starlight glistens and gleams on the winter snow, while moonbeams shine through the window and dance on the wooden floor.

The window rattles. There is the sound of blowing wind. Then suddenly two tall and wondrous angels appear, shedding light and joy. With gentle touch they gather a child in either arm, kiss each twice, and bear them off to Paradise.

This is Christmas Eve, the Christ Child's birthday, and here beneath the sun-bright brilliance of the Eastern Star the children waken. Before them stands the Holy Child. With innocent delight He greets His playmates, fortunate fellow keepers of His feast.

The merrymaking begins, and never a more joyful party has there been! Such singing and such laughter! The children gasp and race in pursuit of rainbow hoops and golden balls. Starlit twine holds meteoric kites that soar to great heights, and bursting displays of the Milky Way fill the heavens. Throughout the spheres melodious chants are sung by angelic choruses. Thus do all the innocent children span galaxy upon galaxy. Finally, as dawn awaits behind a cloud, the children and their Host blow out each star like candles and the glorious light fades. With strong and gentle grasp, the angels lift their nodding charges and carry them back in sweet sleep to their beds.

Morning breaks. Refreshed and dazzled, the children rush to their parents, carrying tales of wonder. But their speech stumbles and falters, and soon they fall silent. The parents shrug and smile in earthly ignorance, saying, "It was all a dream that soon will be forgotten."

But they are wrong. What the parents cannot hear shall not be lost to the children. Inexpressible though it may be, the joy of the children captured by Christmas shall remain deep in their hearts for all their lives, and they shall grow beautiful and wise.

Christmas with the Goblins

A Folk Tale of Finland

On Christmas Eve, many years ago, there lived two children in Finland named Fredrik and Lotta. Fredrik, who was ten, was stout and noisy, and always seemed to be playing pranks on others. He had, however, been trying to behave himself, for he knew the Yule Goat would soon arrive for his annual Christmas visit. Fredrik's younger sister, Lotta, was also eagerly awaiting the Goat's appearance. The Yule Goat was a gruff old creature, but he always brought many presents to good Finnish children and she was sure she would get at least twenty-five boxes this year. The children paced impatiently about their living room, peering out the windows every few seconds.

Finally, there came a loud knock at the door and, sure enough, in strutted the big, hairy Goat. He gazed down at the two children and asked in a rasping voice if they had been good.

"Oh!" they exclaimed. "Yes!"

"Very well," he replied. "But I must tell you there will be only half as many boxes as usual this year."

"But why?" asked Fredrik and Lotta.

"Well," said the Goat, "on my travels from the far North, I peeped in the doors of many poor cottages and saw so many little children who hadn't even a crust of bread that I gave half of my Christmas boxes to them. Was I not right in doing so?"

"You mean, " cried Fredrik, "I will only get half of what I got last year? Why, even the goblins will have a better Christmas than I."

"Yes, indeed," pouted Lotta. "It does seem the goblins are better off than we are tonight."

"Very well," sniffed the old Yule Goat, "if you think so, I will take you to the goblins at once." Saying this, he seized Fredrik and Lotta and carried them off, in spite of their struggles to get loose.

On and on they went, quick as lightening, when suddenly the children found themselves all alone in the middle of a large forest. Snow was all about, they were frightfully cold, and close by they heard the wolves howl. They both began to scream and cry, but the more they shouted the nearer the wolves came.

"Come, Lotta," yelled Fredrik, "we must run for shelter."

"This way," she cried, "I think I saw a light."

They scrambled through huge snowdrifts, over fallen trees and bushes, and soon came to the bottom of a towering, icy mountain. In the mountainside they discovered a little door, with faint light leaking from its cracked opening. They pushed it open further and tiptoed through. To their amazement they found themselves looking upon a huge and horrid festival. It was too late to turn back, the wolves were scratching at the door behind them.

Full of fear, Fredrik and Lotta gazed into a large dim hall. There were thousands and thousands of goblins and trolls, wrinkled, hunched, grizzled beings, shrieking and cackling and scuttling about. They carried frozen glow-worms on rotten twigs, which cast a dull, phosphorescent light in the dark. Should one want to make a grand light, he would stroke a large black cat along the back until sparks flashed out. But then many others would shriek, "Stop! Stop! It is far too light; no one can stand such a glare!"

Now one of the strange things about trolls and goblins is that they hate light. This was why they were holding such a feast right then, for they had observed the days were becoming shorter and shorter, and the nights longer and longer. They thought, as they do every year, that at last there would be no more day, only one great, black night. (For trolls and goblins, like people, are inclined to believe whatever they wish will happen.) And so they were wildly happy, and they danced and screamed in the mountain, keeping a merry Christmas in a most heathen fashion.

The goblin mountain was ruled by Mundus, the king of darkness, who was now sitting in the midst of the hall. By his side was the troll queen, Caro, who had a long and skimpy beard just like the evil king's. The two of them chewed on fern and spiders' legs, and sipped on ice crystals, greatly enjoying the festivities about them.

Then King Mundus arose from his throne and began a grand speech. "Behold!" he thundered, "light will soon be at an end and the shadows of darkness will spread forever over the world. And the trolls and the goblins shall have all the power."

"Hurrah," shouted the grisly creatures. "Long live our king and queen! Hurrah! Darkness forever!"

Fredrik and Lotta shuddered to hear the frightful cheers, dreading whatever might happen next.

The king then said, "Where is my chief watchman, whom I sent to the top of the mountain to see if any light remains in the world?"

The watchman came and said, "Sir King, your power is great. Darkness reigns."

"Return to the mountain top," the pleased king said.

After a while Mundus asked again, "Where is my watchman?" and the watchman came.

"Sir King," the watchman was perplexed. "There is a faint star on the horizon."

The king frowned. "Go back again," he said.

Shortly, the king spoke again, "Where is my watchman?"

But now, the watchman trembled, and one could see he was quite blind.

"What is it?" Mundus cried.

The watchman answered, "Sir King, the clouds have lifted, and a star, larger and brighter than any other, beams in the endless sky."

"What does this mean?" the king roared.

And then he saw the trembling children, and cried, "Bring those two to me!"

Poor Fredrik and Lotta quaked and shook and could barely swallow, they were so frightened.

"Now," the king said, "you are in my power. I can change you to crows, or spiders perhaps. But I will give you a riddle instead. Answer it truly, and you will have your freedom. Do you agree to this?"

"Yes," the children gulped and gasped.

"Now," shrieked the king madly, "why is it that such a bright star rises in the darkest night of the year, when darkness and trolldom should reign?"

"It is the Christmas star, that rises over Bethlehem," Lotta answered.

"Why does it shine so?" The king asked.

"Because this night our Saviour is born, and He is the Light that lights up the whole world," said Fredrik.

The king began to shake violently, and asked again, "And what is this Saviour's name?"

Both the children answered, "Jesus Christ, who brings love and forgiveness to all mankind." As they spoke, a peacefulness descended in their hearts.

But the mountain began to shake and fall apart. A stormwind rushed through the hall.

All the trolls and goblins disappeared like shadows and smoke, and the ice began to glitter and melt and crackle and shatter.

That was the last the children remembered of Mundus and the mountain and all the glaring trolls and goblins. The next they knew, Kajea, their kind-hearted old nurse, was by their beds urging, "Wake up, my sleepyheads, it is Christmas, and time to go to church."

And go to church they did, where all was bright and beautiful. And they were so glad to be there they did not miss getting their Christmas boxes at all. And though they never, in all their lives, mentioned the goblin's Christmas to another living soul (except many years later when Lotta told her great-grandchild, who told the tale to me), they learned to keep Christmas in their hearts, where it belonged, and to show love and kindness to everyone, and to share what they had with those who had less.

The Legend of the Cat

Legend tells of how, on the first Christmas Eve when the holy Babe lay in His Bethlehem crib, a strange and wonderful thing happened throughout fields and forests. All the wild creatures, all the beasts and all the birds, left their lairs and their nests and travelled in silent wonder to pay homage to the Lord.

Cat came, too. Shy and wild, from the nightly depths of the forest, Cat came. With arched back, soundless step, and staring eyes he came and curled no closer than the warmth of the hearth. There he lay, silent and distant, while all the other creatures bowed down together in peaceful reverence, the lion and deer, the eagle and hare, the fox and field mouse. Cat, overcome by glory, could only gaze at the Baby's bed, could not bow his head, and a low, trembling sound grew from deep in his throat.

As morning dawned, a sense of sameness returned. One by one the creatures fled. Except Cat. He remained, unable to quit the crib and hearth, unable to come closer. Mary's voice broke the silence.

"Dear Cat," she said, "dear proud, stubborn, stiff-necked Cat, bless you. Now, leave wilderness behind. By no force, you have stayed. The hearth has bound you to itself. From this hour, you shall be where Man is, fond and free. And your pulsing, household humming shall bring warmth to many a family."

And so it has been. Some winter nights, vague jungle stirrings gleam in Cat's eyes. His back arches, claws stretch and scratch at the remembrance. But the dream flees, and Cat curls, reassured and content, upon his human hearth.

Christmas Poem

Eugene Field

Why do bells for Christmas ring?
Why do little children sing?

Once a lovely, shining star,
Seen by shepherds from afar,
Gently moved until its light
Made a manger's cradle bright.

There a darling baby lay,
Pillowed soft upon the hay;
And its mother sang and smiled,
"This is Christ, the holy child."

Therefore bells for Christmas ring,
Therefore little children sing.

The Christmas Rose

"And there were in the same country shepherds abiding in the field, keeping watch over their flock by night.

And, lo, the angel of the Lord came upon them, and the glory of the Lord shone round about them: and they were sore afraid.

And the angel said unto them, Fear not: for behold, I bring you good tidings of great joy, which shall be to all people.

For unto you is born this day in the city of David a Saviour, which is Christ the Lord.

And this shall be a sign unto you; Ye shall find the Babe wrapped in swaddling clothes, lying in a manger.

And suddenly there was with the angel a multitude of the heavenly host praising God, and saying,

Glory to God in the highest, and on earth peace, good will toward men."

St. Luke II:8-14

The angels disappeared. A great confusion and commotion began among the shepherds. Amidst cries of wonder and astonishment, each was looking about his goods for a gift suitable to bring the baby King. Offerings of bread, blankets, wool and lambs were gathered as the shepherds prepared to visit the manger. Only a very small, very young shepherdess stood still and silent by the flocks of sheep.

With her tattered shawl wrapped tightly about her thin shoulders, the little girl gazed sadly at the backs of the sheep. She had no family, no one to help her prepare a gift for the baby Jesus. Still, she longed to see this wondrous Child. Even without a gift, she decided, she would go to the Bethlehem stable. Hopefully, no one would notice her. The warm, woolly smell and low baaing of the sheep made her feel better.

The lowly stable was not far. The shepherds approached quietly, joyfully. There, lying upon the sweet-smelling hay, was the tender Babe, only hours old, pink and rosy and all warmly wrapped in swaddling clothes. His eyes were closed. The soft murmurings of His breath made Him seem asleep, and a warm glow filled the wooden shed.

The little girl's heart swelled at the sight of Him, so small and sweet and tender. Oh, how she longed to give Him something. He was so beautiful, her eyes filled with tears. One teardrop spilled over, ran down her faint cheek and splashed to the ground. She looked down and beheld, at her feet, a pale flower where the tear had fallen. Gladly, she picked it and went to lay it down by the Child's head. As she approached, the Baby's eyes blinked. His tiny fingers reached up and touched the flower, which turned a blushing rose pink, a Christmas rose.

The two children, One in the manger and one by His side, gazed joyfully at each other. The little girl touched the flower. In her heart she knew it was the least of the miracles that happened that night.

The Legend of the Spiders

Many, many Christmas Eves ago, in a certain house in a little town in Germany, it was customary for all the house animals to gather after the family was in bed and view the Christmas tree (which was, of course, decorated from top to bottom with beautiful, sparkling lights and glistening glass balls).

And so, when the last footstep had sounded on the upstairs floor, and deep, sleepy snores filled the bedrooms, the creatures gathered around the twinkling tree. The yellow canary chirped and warbled in wonder, flitting brightly from branch to branch. The aloof tabby at first lounged about licking its paws, but was soon prowling intently beneath the glimmering tree, eyes round and shining with obvious delight. The family dog gazed contentedly at the happy sight, and even the shy, little mice scuttled in for a merry peek.

In this manner, all the creatures of the house appeared. All except the small gray spiders. And where were they? Well, the house mother (a neat and tidy woman) had no use for spiders. She was continually going around with a big broom, sweeping things up, so the spiders had to run off double quick. It was only in the most remote nooks and crannies of the house that the spiders were even close to being safe.

But the spiders longed to see the marvelous tree, the beautiful tree all bright and shining. So they complained to the Christ Child (who loves all creatures, even the homeliest and most humble), and the Christ Child let them in to see the tree when everyone else was gone.

What a time they had! They all came . . . creepy, creepy, creepy . . . from the attic and the cellar, up the walls and along the halls, and into the beautiful room. Dainty little mama spiders and big proud papa spiders and teensy weensy baby spiders and respected old grandpa spiders all came and looked. Such a marvelous sight! And then, they began to climb, branch to branch, needle to needle, ball to ball. To the very tip top star and down again they went, creepy, crawly, in and out, right up close to every pretty little thing they could see.

Finally, they were done. Slowly, silently, contentedly, they crept down and disappeared — vanished — just like that! But the tree — it was now covered with cobwebs — dull, gray cobwebs from top to bottom! Not a twig had the little spiders missed.

Now the Christ Child knew well how the house mother disliked cobwebs, and He knew how much the children would be disappointed to find their tree, so carefully decorated, covered with the dull webs. And He loved them all, too. So He leaned and touched the webs and in a brief moment they all turned to shimmering silver, like glimmering icicles. Never, in all time, had there been such a tree, and it was hard to say who had been more excited to see it, all the little spiders or the children when they awoke on Christmas morning.

Christmas at the Hollow Tree Inn

Albert Bigelow Paine

Once upon a time, when the Robin, and Turtle, and Squirrel, and Jack Rabbit had all gone home for the winter, nobody was left in the Hollow Tree except the Raccoon and 'Possum and the old black Crow. Of course the others used to come back and visit, and Mr. Dog, too, now that he had got to be good friends with all the Deep Woods people. Mr. Dog told them a lot of things they had never heard of before, things that he'd learned at Mr. Man's house.

He told them about Santa Claus, and how the old fellow came down the chimney on Christmas Eve to bring presents to Mr. Man and his children, who always hung up their stockings for them, and Mr. Dog said that once he had hung up his stocking, too, and got a nice bone in it. He said that Santa Claus always came to Mr. Man's house, and that whenever the children hung up their stockings they were always sure to get something in them.

Well, the Hollow Tree people had never heard of Santa Claus. You see, Santa Claus only comes to Mr. Man's house, but they didn't know that, so they thought if they hung up their stockings he'd come there, too, and that's what they made up their minds to do. Mr. 'Possum looked over all of his stockings to pick out the biggest one, and Mr. Crow made himself a new pair on purpose. Mr. Raccoon said he never knew Mr. Crow to make himself such big stockings before, but Mr. Crow said he was getting old and needed things bigger, and when he loaned one of his new stockings to Mr. Raccoon, Mr. Raccoon said, "That's so," and that he guessed they were all right after all. They didn't tell anyone about it at first, but by and by they told Mr. Dog what they were going to do, and when Mr. Dog heard he wanted to laugh right out. You see, he knew Santa Claus never went anywhere except to Mr. Man's house and he thought it would be a great joke on the Hollow Tree people when they hung up their stockings and didn't get anything.

But by and by, Mr. Dog thought it would be too bad for them to be disappointed. You see, Mr. Dog liked them all and when he had thought about it a minute he made up his mind to play Santa Claus!

He knew just how Santa Claus looked, 'cause he'd seen his pictures at Mr. Man's house, and he thought it would be great fun to dress up and take a bag of presents to the Hollow Tree and fill up those stockings. But first he had to find a way of getting in, so he said to them he didn't see how they could expect Santa, their chimneys were so small, and Mr. Crow said they could leave their latchstring out, which was just what Mr. Dog wanted. Then they asked Mr. Dog to Christmas dinner, if he could get away, to see what presents they got in their stockings. Mr. Dog said he'd come and went off laughing to himself.

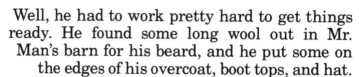

Well, he had to work pretty hard to get things ready. He found some long wool out in Mr. Man's barn for his beard, and he put some on the edges of his overcoat, boot tops, and hat. Then he borrowed a big sack and filled it with nice things.

He had some new neckties for the Hollow Tree people, and big, striped candy canes, and a new pipe for each, and a package of tobacco. And then he started out all dressed up like Santa Claus with his bag slung over his shoulder.

His bag got heavier and heavier and he was glad to get to the Hollow Tree and find the latchstring out. He set his bag down to rest a minute and listened. All he could hear was Mr. Crow, Mr. Raccoon and Mr. 'Possum breathing pretty low, and he knew they might wake up any minute so he slipped into the parlor. When he got up there he almost had to laugh right out, for there were the stockings, all hung up in a row, and a card with a name on each one.

He opened his bag and filled the stockings with mixed candy and nuts and the pipes and tobacco and candy canes. I tell you, they looked fine! He forgot about anyone waking and sat down in a nice rocking chair in the corner to look at the stockings. He thought how pleased they'd be in the morning and how tired he was. You've heard about people being as tired as a dog; and that's just how Mr. Dog felt. By and by, he went sound asleep right there in his chair, with all his Santa Claus clothes on.

There he sat, all night long, and even when it came morning he slept right on. Then pretty soon Mr. 'Possum poked his head out, then Mr. Crow and Mr. Raccoon did, too. They all looked toward the stockings, and they didn't see Mr. Dog, or even each other. They saw their stockings, though, and Mr. Raccoon said all at once:

"Oh, there's something in my stocking!"

And Mr. Crow says: "Oh, there's something in my stocking, too!"

And Mr. 'Possum says: "Oh, there's something in all our stockings!"

And with that they all gave a great hurrah together, and rushed out and grabbed their stockings and turned around just in time to see Mr. Dog jump straight up out of his chair, for he did not know where he was the least bit in the world.

"Oh, there's Santa Claus himself!" they all shouted together, and made a rush for their rooms, for they were scared almost to death. But it all dawned on Mr. Dog in a second, and he began to laugh to think what a joke it was on everybody. And when they heard Mr. Dog laugh they knew him right away and they all came up and he had to tell just what he'd done; so they emptied their stockings and ate some of the presents and looked at others, until they almost forgot about breakfast, just as children do on Christmas morning.

Then Mr. Crow said he'd make a little coffee and that Mr. Dog must stay and have some, and by and by they made him promise to spend the day with them. It was snowing hard outside and it snowed so hard that Mr. Dog decided to stay all night and after dinner they all sat around the fire and told stories. And Mr. Crow and Mr. 'Possum and Mr. Raccoon had the very nicest Christmas that ever was in the Hollow Tree or in the Big Deep Woods anywhere.

BABOUSCKA

The Legend of Babouscka

There is a tale told in Russia of a very old woman who lived a long, long time ago. Her name was Babouscka, and her home was a little hut in the coldest corner of that cold, cold country. Here the winter wind rattled loudly at her windows and piled deep snow drifts round about her cozy little house. And though Babouscka lived where four roads met, in the months when the snow flew, not a soul had ever passed her door.

Babouscka worked hurriedly those days, sweeping her bare floor, baking bread and tidying her hut as best she could. She was lonely. Her heart longed for summer's warmth, the songs of the birds and sweet fragrances of the wild flowers. Now she was anxious to finish her day's work so she might go to sleep beneath her warm quilts and dream of better times.

Then one night, in the gloomy dusk, a most strange thing happened. Babouscka heard, far off, the tink, tink, tinkling of bells and the vague sounds of distant voices. She peered out her frost-laced window. Down the widest and loneliest of the snow-covered roads, she could just barely see a large procession of people. As they drew closer, she could hear dismay and anger in their voices. Jangling camelbells crackled in the cold, crisp air. But strangest of all were the three men astride the humped beasts. Indeed, these were kings, Babouscka thought. They wore magnificent crowns, the jewels of their breastplates gleamed in the fading light, their heavy fur wraps were thick and warm, and each was attended by many servants.

Babouscka caught her breath. They were stopping before her hut. There was an impatient knock at the door. She was slow to answer. What could such persons want of her? As she cracked open her door the wind, whistling and howling, invaded her snug home. She peered suspiciously at the strangers. The servants noisily asked her for directions to some strange place of which she'd never heard. She shook her head dumbly. With scolding looks, they repeated their questions. But Babouscka's confusion only grew. Seeing this, one of the kings bid the servants hold their tongues, and spoke kindly to Babouscka.

"We are on a long journey, for we have seen a wondrous star in the sky. It leads to a town where a newborn child lies, and it is for Him that we search. But now the star is blocked by clouds. Can you at least show us the way to the next village?"

"Who is this child?"

"A King, and we go to worship Him. Come with us, Babouscka. Such a child there has never been."

Babouscka peered into the dark, cheerless night. The warmth of her home beat on her back. This star was nowhere to be seen. The bitter wind howled again. She shivered and shook her head no, no she couldn't go. Not now. Perhaps tomorrow.

But the three kings could not wait for an old woman to make up her mind. By the next day's sun they were far ahead on their journey, and even the tracks of the camels had been swept beneath the deep snow.

As the days passed, poor Babouscka thought a great deal about the kings, of their glory and of their vision of the little baby. She had no children, no one to love, no one to love her. The more she thought of this, the more her heart hurt. Ah, she sighed, if only she had gone with them!

Day by day her regret grew over the chance she had missed. The child became her first and only thought. Finally, the very sight of her home became hateful to her. One day she could stand it no longer. She wrapped herself in her warmest shawl, filled her basket with her best goods and shut the door of her house behind her forever.

Babouscka had no hope of overtaking the three kings. But she thought she might find the child they had sought so that she, too, might love and worship Him. And so her journey began.

It is said in Russia that it still continues, that all through the winter months Babouscka travels across fields and through villages in search of the Holy Child born in Bethlehem so many years ago. In the late nights, when tired mothers sleep, she tiptoes into nurseries and longingly peeks beneath the blankets that cover the sleeping children. With her brown, wrinkled face close to the pillow she looks kindly. Her eyes are moist as she lays the coverlet down again and slips away in silence. And always she leaves behind a candy or trinket, something she hopes will lighten the heart of the little child she's left.

It is said by some that Babouscka's journey is one of sorrow and regret, that her search will never be satisfied. But others believe that Babouscka knows the Christ Child can no longer be found in one human child, but is in all children. For Babouscka, He is in each one to whom she gives her gifts, and while the searching never ends, neither does the finding. So Babouscka will always search, and she will always find, and her place will always be among all living children.